DETECTIVE
THOMAS
AND THE
BIGGEST
QUESTION

Caitlin E. Bootsma

Illustrations by Evie Schwartzbauer

Nihil Obstat
Msgr. Michael Heintz, Ph.D.
Censor Librorum

Imprimatur
✠ Kevin C. Rhoades
Bishop of Fort Wayne-South Bend
December 9, 2022

The *Nihil Obstat* and *Imprimatur* are official declarations that a book is free from doctrinal or moral error. It is not implied that those who have granted the *Nihil Obstat* and *Imprimatur* agree with the contents, opinions, or statements expressed.

Except where noted, the Scripture citations used in this work are taken from the *Revised Standard Version of the Bible — Second Catholic Edition* (Ignatius Edition), copyright © 1965, 1966, 2006 National Council of the Churches of Christ in the United States of America. Used by permission. All rights reserved.

Every reasonable effort has been made to determine copyright holders of excerpted materials and to secure permissions as needed. If any copyrighted materials have been inadvertently used in this work without proper credit being given in one form or another, please notify Our Sunday Visitor in writing so that future printings of this work may be corrected accordingly.

Copyright © 2023 by Caitlin E. Bootsma

28 27 26 25 24 23   1 2 3 4 5 6 7 8 9

All rights reserved. With the exception of short excerpts for critical reviews, no part of this work may be reproduced or transmitted in any form or by any means whatsoever without permission from the publisher. For more information, visit: www.osv.com/permissions.

Our Sunday Visitor Publishing Division
Our Sunday Visitor, Inc.
200 Noll Plaza
Huntington, IN 46750
1-800-348-2440

ISBN: 978-1-63966-011-7 (Inventory No. T2750)
LCCN: 2023900779

Cover and interior design: Lindsey Riesen
Cover and interior art: Evelyn Schwartzbauer

1. JUVENILE FICTION—Religious—Christian—Mysteries & Detective Stories.
2. JUVENILE FICTION—Religious—Christian—General.
3. RELIGION—Christianity—Catholic.

PRINTED IN THE UNITED STATES OF AMERICA

For Gus, whose biggest question at a young age inspired this book. May you always seek the truth with both your mind and your soul.

Contents

Chapter 1

An Unanswered Question

"I ... don't ... know," Thomas said for the first time ever.

He sat down with a plop.

The rest of the kids in his religious education class were as surprised as he was. Eleven-year-old Thomas always had the answer, and if he didn't, he found it out. He was so good at finding things out that he considered himself a detective.

But this was one mystery he couldn't crack on his own.

Why did he, Thomas, personally believe in God? That was the question the teacher had asked. Thomas, who *always* had something to say, was at a loss for words. He did believe in God, but he didn't really know *why*.

He walked slowly from the classroom to the church for Mass, still thinking about this problem. *Why do I actually believe God exists?*

Suddenly, the wind picked up. Thomas felt a chill.

"Not again!" Thomas shivered, thinking regretfully of the jacket he'd left in the classroom. Let's just say that forgetting things was the norm for Thomas. He spent so much time thinking about life's big questions that he often forgot practical things — like jackets. His parents, teachers, and, well, everyone, called him absent-minded.

After running back to get his jacket, Thomas scooted into the pew next to his parents, younger brother, and sister, just as the priest reached the front of the church.

He tried to focus on praying — he really did. He did pretty well through the readings and the good-but-somewhat-long homily ... but then ...

Thomas stood up to pray the Creed, just like he did every Sunday: "I believe in God the Father almighty, maker of heaven and earth ... "

He stopped and nudged his dad in the ribs.

"Dad, why do we believe God created heaven and earth?"

"Ouch! Stop that, Thomas. Can we talk about this later?"

Thomas was quiet for a minute, but then started whispering, "I know we believe in God, but *how* do we know that He exists? How come I don't know?"

His dad gave him a look that said, "We'll talk about this later. Right now, we need to pray." Thomas sighed.

He sat down for the Offertory as his younger siblings, Charlie and Anna, squabbled over who was going to put money in the collection plate. Nine-year-old Charlie managed to squeeze himself into the aisle and joyfully plunked his change in, while seven-year-old Anna gave up and waited for the usher to pass by.

Mass ended, and it was time for donuts and tree-climbing. Thomas shoved the question of God's existence into the back of his ever-moving brain.

That afternoon in his Richmond, Virginia, neighborhood, Thomas packed up his baseball gear after the game. The Lightning Bolts had won today — for the first time ever — so the team was in a good mood.

"How has your weekend been? Do anything fun?" his teammate Mateo asked, shoving his mitt into his bag.

"Nothing much. Yesterday I helped my dad with gardening, took my sister to the park ..."

Thomas purposefully didn't mention going to Mass

that morning. His Catholic faith was a big part of his life, but he felt embarrassed to tell his teammate about it.

Something nagged at him as he turned to walk away. Taking a deep breath, he turned back to Mateo to add, "Oh yeah, and we went to church this morning, like we always do."

Phew, he said to himself, *that wasn't so hard.*

"We go to church sometimes, too," his friend Nate chimed in. That made Thomas feel a bit less weird.

"You go to Mass every week? Why bother?" Mateo interrupted. Mateo was just a little intimidating — a head taller than everyone else on the team and easily the most talented player.

Thomas gulped. His hands suddenly felt a little sweaty. He wanted to be honest about what he believed, but he *also* wanted to impress Mateo, because Thomas always felt like Mateo was cooler than he was.

He took a deep breath. "Well, we're Catholic, and it's important to us."

Mateo pushed. "But you can't even know God actually exists, so why spend time in a stuffy church instead of having fun?"

Here it was again — the question he couldn't answer. Why did he believe in God? How could anyone know for sure that God exists?

Was it possible that Mateo had a point?

Thomas had been going to Mass his whole life. He was baptized and received his first Communion. He prayed with his family and by himself. Sometimes, he even read the Bible. Thomas believed that God is the Creator of the universe and loves each one of us. But he couldn't explain *why* he believed it.

"I'll get back to you on that ..." Thomas mumbled, slinging his bag over his shoulder.

"Let me know what you come up with," said Mateo with a bit of a sneer, laughing to his teammates as Thomas retreated.

In the front seat of the minivan, Thomas's dad was ready to talk about the game — who the MVP was, what the team did well, and how they could be better. But for the second time that day, Thomas was uncharacteristically silent.

He had questions!

Why did he believe God is real? Does it make sense to think God exists? Why couldn't he be more confident about his faith around other people? Why should he even care what Mateo thought?

Thomas took a deep breath and decided that it was time to approach these questions like the mysteries they were. Detective Thomas was on the case!

Chapter 2
A Not-So-Simple Mystery

Thomas had an impressive talent. You see, Thomas really was a detective. He solved lots of mysteries at school and at home. Thomas knew how to figure out problems.

He kept all his solved mysteries in a series of beat-up notebooks. Occasionally, his family would look over his shoulder at whatever he was working on. They'd even help with the cases sometimes!

That afternoon, he pulled the notebooks off the shelf in his room and read through his past cases. The pages were full of messy notes, highlighted questions, and photo evidence pasted in.

SOLVED

* The mystery of the hole-filled house. Was it a robber with a drill? A neighbor throwing rocks? No, it was ... a woodpecker!

* The mystery of Sarah-Beth's missing report. She couldn't find her tundra diorama (a decorated shoe box) presentation anywhere! Did the janitor throw it out by accident? Did another student steal it and use it as their own? It turns out her little sister Kelly had taken it to the attic to use it as a new adventure setting for her dolls!

* The mystery of the lost purse. Thomas discovered that it wasn't lost, it was stolen right out of their car one night!

How can we know God exists? Thomas wondered. He turned to a new page in a notebook and titled it "The Biggest Question." After all, what could be more important to figure out? He was sure this wouldn't be an easy case, but he was up for the challenge.

He realized he really cared about solving this mystery. Mateo didn't think people could really know that God exists, but Thomas did. The more he thought about it, the more he realized it was a crucial part of being Christian. How could he really say he believed in God if he couldn't even explain why he believed in Him?

At dinner time, Thomas bounded into the dining room and jumped right in:

"Dad, I was trying to ask you at Mass ... how do we know God exists?"

Dad, always the scientist, replied as he handed Thomas a plate, "Just look at the world around you! There are clues in the food chain, in the way flowers are made, and in how unique each one of us is!"

"What kind of clues?"

"Well, first of all, we know that we didn't create ourselves. Our world is so complex, so well-designed, it had to come from a Creator!"

"Huh," Thomas said. "So, you're saying there is no way everything in creation just came out of nowhere?"

"Exactly!" his dad said.

"That's right," his mom chimed in. Mom taught religion at the high school, so this was her specialty.

"We can also use our minds to understand why God's existence makes sense."

"OK, but I'm not sure I know where to start ..." Thomas trailed off.

"I know God exists!" Anna enthusiastically contributed.

"Oh yeah?" Thomas asked. "How?"

"I pray to Him, and He answers me in my heart," she replied.

Thomas didn't really know what to say to that, but she had a point. Still, Thomas wanted proof. He wanted to be able to answer the question in a way that made sense to his teammates.

"Charlie, anything to add?" his dad asked, trying to include Thomas's brother.

"Nope," said Charlie briefly, looking up from his third hot dog and the comic book he was secretly reading under the table.

"CHARLIE!" the rest of the family exclaimed.

Charlie acted like all he cared about was food and graphic novels, but Thomas always felt like Charlie was paying more attention to the conversation than he seemed to be.

Later that night, Thomas drifted off to sleep puzzling over these questions.

His dreams went in a million different directions.

Charlie pulling a funny prank on him on vacation ...

Christmas, seeing Jesus in a manger, and opening presents — a new baseball! A video game! ...

His little sister, born when he was just a little kid himself ...

Kneeling in church, thanking God for all these blessings ...

Mateo and the other kids laughing at him ...

He woke up with a start.

Catching his breath after that crazy night of dreams, he got up to get dressed.

The light from the window was shining brightly on his dresser. When he opened a drawer to grab a pair of pants, he gasped in surprise. Sitting among his clothes was a small box that looked like it was made of pure gold.

Dear Thomas,
asking questions
is a good thing.
A famous philosopher
named Aristotle
said this.

Chapter 3
The Moving Ball

*W*ell, *that's weird*, Thomas said to himself. *It's not my birthday, and this doesn't look like anything I've ever seen before!*

It was no bigger than a lunch box. Thomas picked up the box and examined it. It looked like a gold chest from a museum, but it was surprisingly light.

Is it possible this is meant for me? he wondered. As if in answer, the box suddenly sprang open!

Inside, he found an ancient-looking piece of paper. The writing on it didn't look like the cursive they learned in school. It was much fancier and seemed like it had been written with a feather pen.

OK, Thomas thought, *this is definitely strange.*

He concentrated to decipher the unfamiliar lettering.

Dear Thomas,

Asking questions is a good thing. A famous philosopher from Ancient Greece, named Aristotle, said this: "All men by nature desire to know." That means questioning things and searching for answers is part of who you are! And knowing that God exists is a particularly important mystery to solve.

I've spent a lot of time thinking about God's existence. In fact, I developed some strong arguments for

it based on things we can observe in the world around us. I want to share with you five ways we can know that God exists. These are called "proofs," because we can prove that they are true.

We'll work through them one by one. Here's what you need to do:

· Each time you are ready to explore a new proof of God's existence, come to this box.

· Open the box to find an object and a clue. They will help guide you.

· Think about the clue throughout the day; write down your observations.

· When you think you've found the answer, write it down and place the note back in the box.

· Close the box and repeat.

Are you ready?

Signed,
T. A.

P.S. Don't let other kids decide what you believe.
Let their doubt be your motivation to discover the truth!

"OK," Thomas said out loud as he closed the box. "Is someone playing some sort of trick on me? How do they know about my questions about God? And who is T. A.?"

Thomas was still confused about whether this was a joke, but he did really want to figure out whether God exists. He was an amateur[1] detective, after all!

---

1. That's detective-speak for a "beginner"!

Thomas was eager to jump right in to T.A.'s instructions, but there was something he felt compelled to do first.

He got down on his knees to pray. It didn't seem like the time for an Our Father or a Hail Mary, so he decided to wing it.

He made the Sign of the Cross:

In the name of the Father and of the Son and of the Holy Spirit. Amen.

Then he folded his hands together, closed his eyes, and prayed:

"Uh ... hi, God. Will You help me on my quest? I *believe* that You are real, but I really want to *know* it. You know? OK, thank You. Amen."

He stood up, a little nervous, and opened the box again.

The original letter was gone. A new note was in its place with the same old-fashioned handwriting. Beside it, there was a baseball (that was clearly *not* new) sporting some dirt from a lot of baseball games.

The note read:

Dear Thomas,

Can you think of something that changes? Change can be when anything moves, takes on a new form, or grows (to name just a few kinds of change). Do things change completely by themselves, or does something else change them?

Consider this baseball. Does it move by itself? If not, what moves it?

Now let's go back another step. What moves or changes the thing that moves the ball?

What moves or changes that thing?

You can keep asking this question over and over, creating a "chain" of earlier changes. But eventually, *you'll have to get to the beginning — to the first person or thing that ever moved or changed anything. Who or what is that? That is the Original Mover.*

Write down your observations.

T. A.

Thomas looked at the baseball. *Can this baseball move without help?* he wondered.

That seemed like a silly question, but he was ready to follow the clue and see what the day brought.

"Time for breakfast!" Mom called up the stairs, interrupting his thoughts.

He grabbed the baseball. As he ran down the hall, he poked his head into the living room to check on Roley the fish. Roley didn't seem particularly active that morning, but Thomas had bigger things on his mind.

Reality Detective Lab

Can you solve the mystery before Thomas? Start your own observation notebook and see if these questions can help you solve the clues. If you get stuck, invite your parents or an older sibling to complete the questions with you!

1. Can you think of something that moves?

2. Does it move itself or does something cause it to move?

3. If something else causes it to move, what causes that thing to move? How far back can you trace the cause of movements?

4. How do you think the moving baseball will help Thomas understand God's existence?

Mom was pulling eggs out of the fridge to cook, so Thomas grabbed a fork and plopped down at the table with his baseball.

The baseball sat there on the counter. Not moving.

Thomas gave it a little push. Of course, it moved!

"Aha!" Thomas yelled, startling his mom and sister. "Uh, sorry guys!" Thomas sank into his chair sheepishly. "I'm solving a mystery and just saw the first clue in action."

"Good morning to you, too, Thomas." Mom rolled her eyes good-naturedly as she pulled out the juice glasses.

"Whoops, forgot my notebook." Thomas climbed the stairs two at a time, grabbed his notebook and a pen, tore the covers off Charlie's bed so that he would wake up, ran back downstairs, and started to write.

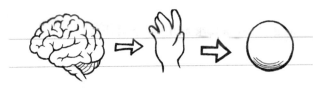

OBSERVATIONS

A ball can't move itself. Either my hand moves it or something else does — like a bat.

He thought for a moment.

My hand moves the ball, but it's my brain that sends the signals for my hand to move.

OK, Thomas thought, *I get it, I think. ... The ball doesn't move itself: my hand moves it. But my hand doesn't move itself either — my brain moves my hand.*

He looked up at his mom standing by the stove. Then it hit him. Eggs are something that change, too! "Mom, can you show me how you cook eggs?"

"Well, sure, this must be my lucky day! I didn't know you were interested in cooking."

Thomas wasn't that interested in cooking, but he did want to learn more about how things changed. He leaned against the counter with his notebook.

"OK, first, I get a pan and put it on the stove," Thomas's mom said as she got the frying pan out of the cabinet.

"Next, I turn the stove on so that the pan is hot. I put a little butter onto the hot pan so the egg won't stick — and because it tastes good. Then I crack the egg so that it changes from something squishy and raw to something fried and delicious."

"Wow, thanks, Mom!" Thomas said, scribbling furiously as the egg turned brown and crispy along the edges.

"You're welcome, Thomas." His mom smiled. "I think we may have just discovered our new morning chef!"

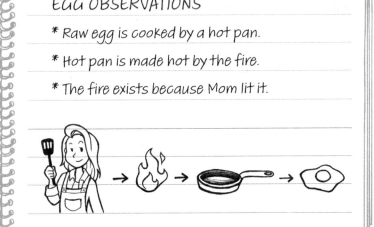

EGG OBSERVATIONS

* Raw egg is cooked by a hot pan.

* Hot pan is made hot by the fire.

* The fire exists because Mom lit it.

Conclusion: Everything that changes is caused by something else!

OK, Thomas thought, closing his notebook. *I sort of understand this chain reaction of changes. Things don't just change themselves. What I'm not so sure of is what this has to do with God's existence.*

Thomas got so lost in thought that he forgot about his delicious-smelling eggs. How could he make the connection between the baseball and God?

Chapter 4
Who Art in Heaven

The sound of his mother's voice made him jump. "THOMAS! CHARLIE!" she yelled from the garage. "It's time to get going to school!"

Thomas hastily placed his dishes in the dishwasher, then crammed the gold box and his notebook and pen into his backpack.

From the corner of his eye, he saw the fish food on

the counter, but as he was about to feed Roley, Charlie yelled, "Beat you to the middle seat!"

Thomas ran for it, leaving the fish food behind. Charlie tripped Thomas, which totally wasn't fair. But Thomas won anyway.

Happily seated in the victory seat, Thomas thought about all the clues he had already uncovered this morning. He was excited by how much he had learned, but he didn't have it all figured out yet.

His heart pounded with excitement. Today would be a busy day for Detective Thomas.

"OK, guys," Mom said once they were on the road, "let's start our day with our prayer."

"OK," said Anna from the back seat.

"Sure," replied Charlie, "but then I have to finish my homework."

"You haven't done your homework yet?!" Mom exclaimed. Irritated, she paused a moment. "Thomas, are you ready?"

"Yes, but I just realized something!" Thomas exclaimed. Everyone paused. They were used to Thomas always working out some thought or mystery.

"The car doesn't move itself."

Charlie looked up from his rapidly scribbled homework. "Well, there are self-driving cars!" he chimed in. "But yeah, obviously Mom drives our car. To be more specific, her foot on the pedal and hands on the wheel move the car." Charlie mimicked his mom driving the car. "Of course, Mom can only push the gas and place her hands on the wheel because of the energy she gets from eating and drinking."

Everyone else underestimated Charlie, but Thomas realized just how smart his younger brother really was.

"So what you're saying is ... everything moves because of something else, and even that something else is moved by something?" Thomas asked.

"Sure," Charlie replied with a shrug, looking back down at his work.

His mom interjected, "Well, God doesn't rely on anyone else to be able to do things."

Thomas paused. He hadn't thought of that. "I — I guess that's true."

"*Speaking* of God, let's pray!" Mom suggested, trying to get everyone back on track.

"Our Father who art in heaven, hallowed be Thy name ..."

Suddenly, a new thought struck Thomas. He'd prayed this prayer hundreds of times, but now he realized: God must be pretty amazing if heaven is His home. And people have been saying His name is holy for literally thousands of years. If only Thomas could understand a little more about Him.

His mother interrupted his thoughts. "Thomas, we're here. It's time to get out!" His siblings were already outside. He jumped out of the car. As he adjusted his backpack, he had a vague feeling that he had forgotten to do something important at home, but he couldn't quite remember what it was. Oh, well.

Thomas waved goodbye to his mom and then turned to scan the front of the school for his friends.

"Hey, Tom," his friend Gabriel greeted him with a fist bump as they headed toward the building.

Thomas had known Gabriel as long as he could remember. Their parents were friends from church. Faith was a central part of Gabriel's devout Filipino family. It was a relief to have a friend who understood how important his faith was to him.

Thomas knew he could talk to Gabriel about this new mystery, but after being laughed at by Mateo, he was nervous. "Gabe," Thomas started hesitantly, "have you ever wondered if we can really know if God exists?"

"What do you mean?" Gabriel sounded puzzled. "We know about Him from the Bible, which was written by real people, including people who knew Jesus when He was on earth. Is that what you mean?"

"Sort of," said Thomas. "When I pray, I believe that God hears me. I even sometimes hear Him in my heart prompting me to do the right thing. But ... I guess what I mean is, how do I prove that He's real? Does it even make sense that there is a God?"

"Woah. Those are some big questions for first thing on a Monday morning." Gabriel looked thoughtful as he fumbled with his locker. "Maybe you could ask God to show you. I mean, if He really is all-knowing, He can do that."

Thomas thought of the small gold box in his backpack. Maybe God was already leading him to the answer.

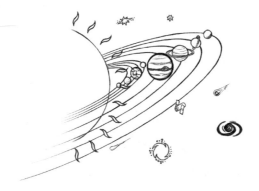

Chapter 5
Planets in Motion

Science class. It was the last class of the morning, and it was usually Thomas's favorite. They got to do experiments, which gave him a chance to practice his detective skills.

"Hey, Church Boy." It was Mateo, of course. Thomas didn't like this new nickname, but he didn't want to get into a fight over it. He ignored Mateo and made his way to his seat.

"All right, class." Mr. Rodriguez pointed to the chalkboard, where he had the solar system mapped out. "We all know that it takes the Earth 365.25 days to go around the sun. But today, we're going to learn more about other planets in motion in our solar system. For example, did you know it takes Jupiter a lot longer than that to make a full orbit? It takes Jupiter 12 *years* to go around the sun!"

Thomas smiled. Mr. Rodriguez was so excited about anything to do with space.

Then it hit him. This was related to the case Thomas was solving! He wrote out some notes in the margin of his science notebook:

My hand rolled the ball this morning. But what keeps these massive planets going around the sun? (Can you imagine trying to push Jupiter around the sun? It's 11 times bigger than Earth!)

Thomas tuned back in to class.

Mr. Rodriguez was explaining: "You see, planets stay in orbit because of the gravitational pull of the sun. The force of gravity is super strong!"

Thomas had his answer. Gravity kept the planets moving in their orbits!

So were the planets part of the chain of moving beings T. A. had written about in his note?

Thomas raised his hand.

"Yes, Thomas?" Mr. Rodriguez responded with a patient smile. He loved that Thomas was always so interested in the mysteries of science.

"I get that gravity keeps planets in orbit. But what makes them move in the first place?" Thomas asked.

"That's a great question, Thomas. The planets were formed out of whirling cloud storms, and they continue to move in the same pattern as those cloud storms."

"But how did the cloud storms start to move?" Thomas asked.

Mr. Rodriguez wasn't sure.

Thomas took out his notebook and wrote:

OBSERVATIONS

* Planets started to move because of a moving cloud storm.

* Planets seem like they move by themselves, but they are really kept in motion by the sun.

* Does something keep the sun burning? I guess burning is how the sun moves or changes. But burning doesn't happen on its own, does it? What started the sun burning?

* Is there anything out there that isn't moved by something else? Who or what is the Original Mover T.A.'s note talked about?

Thomas thought about this for a while. Could God be the Original Mover? Could God be the reason that pans heat up to cook eggs, people drive cars, and planets move?

It made sense: If everything in the universe that moves or changes is moved by something else, eventually we'll find the source of movement.

Nothing changes itself. Eventually, if we keep tracing back all the changes in the universe, there would have to be Someone who started it all and doesn't ever change.

As science class finished, Thomas took the gold box out of his backpack. He opened it up and placed a small scrap of paper in the box. The piece of paper said, in Thomas's messy handwriting,

"God is the Original Mover. God started the process that led to me existing and to moving the baseball."

He closed the box and got ready to open it for the next clue.

RIIINNGGGG

Lunch. He tucked the box under his arm, hoping to find a quiet place in the cafeteria to read the next clue.

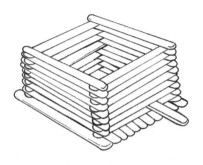

Chapter 6
Popsicle Sticks and the Big Bang

Thomas scanned the lunchroom. Just as he was about to find an empty table, one of the guys from his baseball team called his name. "Hey, Tom! We were just talking about yesterday's game. Come sit with us." Thomas sat.

"Did you see that catch by their third baseman? Wish I could catch like that," one teammate said.

"Ha ha, yeah, but you'd have to be about five inches taller to reach like he did," responded Mateo.

"You did a great job, Tom, catching that fly ball in the 4th inning," another boy commented.

Thomas was hardly listening, still thinking about the clues. "Huh?" he asked absently.

"Don't pay any attention to Tom, guys. He's probably *praying*, since he's so religious," taunted Mateo.

Thomas laughed weakly, but he didn't feel like laughing.

Why was he the only one of his friends who thought about the big questions in life? Even Gabriel, who believed in God, didn't really seem to care why. Maybe Thomas shouldn't care either. It would certainly be easier.

"Hey!" Mateo's voice brought Thomas back to the present. "What's that weird box you're holding? Is it where you keep all your special church things?" Mateo glanced around at the other guys, obviously hoping for another laugh.

Thomas gave a half nod, but then, before he could react, Mateo swooped in and grabbed the box.

"Hey, be careful!"

"What is this?" Mateo stared at the box and opened it up. Inside was the bird feeder Thomas had made as part of a Boy Scout.

As Mateo held out the bird feeder for the rest of the team to see, Thomas saw his chance and grabbed the note from the box. He ignored the other boys, sat down, and started to read.

Thomas,

Great job, detective!
You learned that nothing can change itself. If we follow the chain of changes, we eventually come to

Someone who set that chain in motion — the Original Mover, or God.

This next proof for God's existence can be reasoned out in a similar way. We often refer to God as the "Creator." He is the source of everything that is made. Another term for this is the "First Cause."

Look at your bird feeder. Who made the bird feeder? You did! And who made you? See, we're establishing another chain. Can you trace the bird feeder's creation back to the first Creator?

T. A.

"Hey, Tom! I'm talking to you!" Thomas looked up and saw Mateo throwing the box back and forth with another boy like they were playing catch.

"You said this box was religious. What does a bird

feeder possibly have to do with God?"

Thomas wasn't sure whether Mateo really cared or not, but he paused anyway, gathering his thoughts.

"You asked me at the game why I bothered to go to church. You may have been joking around, but you actually challenged me to think about *why* I believe that God exists."

"And a bird feeder has something to do with figuring that out?" Mateo seemed a little curious.

"Apparently. We can learn a lot about God if we pay attention to the world around us. How things are created, where they come from, all these signs point to the reality of God existing. A bird feeder had to come from somewhere, right?"

"Well yeah, it's made of Popsicle sticks ..." Mateo replied hesitantly, wondering if this was a trick question.

"Right! OK, let's take that a step further. What's a Popsicle stick made of?"

"Wood."

"Yes! This bird feeder wouldn't exist without wood. Where does wood come from?"

Another teammate made a buzzing noise, like a quiz show contestant. "A tree!"

"Exactly!" They were on a roll now. "And trees come from?"

"Seeds," the team chorused back.

"Do you see where this is headed? The bird feeder wouldn't exist without the seed. Everything comes from something else, further and further back on the chain. Nothing makes itself."

Thomas got out his pencil and notebook and scratched a note:

Anything that is made is made by someone or something else. Nothing can be its own cause, because that would be ridiculous.

"Who made that first seed? What is the very First

54

Cause of Everything?"

Mateo was thinking hard. "I know you're thinking the answer is God. But what if the Big Bang started it all? We learned about that in science class."

"That's possible. But where did the Big Bang come from? What caused it?"

"Okay, you got me, Tom" Mateo admitted with uncharacteristically good grace. "Maybe there's a bit more to this God argument than I thought."

His teammates started gathering their lunch trays to return. Mateo paused for a moment. "Um, maybe tell me what else you find out, OK?"

Thomas smiled. "Of course. I'll fill you in at the next game."

Mateo tossed the box back to Thomas, and another teammate handed him the bird feeder.

Reality Detective Lab

1. How would you begin to trace backwards from the creation of the bird feeder?

2. What needed to be created first in that long chain that leads to the creation of the bird feeder?

3. Can you think of something that could exist without a Creator?

4. How do you think the bird feeder will lead Thomas to understand God's existence more?

Thomas turned back to his notebook and wrote:

God is the Creator because He is the First Cause. Ultimately, when you trace it back, God was responsible for the creation of my bird feeder.

He set aside his bird feeder to hang back up in the yard and placed this second proof of God's existence in the box along with the note. They instantly disappeared.

As the bell rang for his next class, Thomas realized he had forgotten to eat lunch. He grabbed a banana from his lunch bag and munched on it as he packed up his stuff and headed to class.

Chapter 7
If THIS, Then THAT

Magnolia Academy was a cool school, as far as schools go. It was a charter school that experimented with different teaching methods that not only taught subjects, but encouraged kids to find solutions for themselves. Thomas's teachers didn't just teach long multiplication and cursive and about computers (though they did that, too). They let kids learn by doing things. Mr. Baker, the math teacher, was the best at this.

"OK, class, put away your books and get ready to explore!"

Thomas glanced at the worksheet with "Logic scavenger hunt" written on it. He loved that learning how to figure out the truth by using reason was a part of math class. One more way to make sense of the universe!

He gave Gabriel a fist bump. "Partners?" With a nod, they quickly exited the classroom.

Last class, they learned about "If, Then" statements, a sort of logical cause and effect. IF we know one thing is true, THEN we can know that something else related is also true.

An example was written on the top of the page. "If it is raining today, then there are clouds in the sky."

I've got this, Thomas thought with a grin as he scanned the list of IF statements.

"Hey, I've found the first one!" Thomas saw that

Gabriel was over at the water fountain pushing the button repeatedly.

"IF I press the button, THEN ..."

"Then water will come out. Check!"

"Hmm, we might have search around a bit for this one. IF the entire floor is wet, THEN ... ?" The boys split up to search the school. Thomas headed upstairs to look in different classrooms. "Come up to the gym!" he called down the stairwell.

Looking at the gleaming gym floor, they began to throw out some ideas.

"If, the entire floor is wet, then ..." began Thomas.

"Someone spilled their water bottle?"

"That's one way for a floor to get wet, but it isn't logical, because the entire floor is wet!"

"OK, if the entire floor is wet, then ... the floor has just been mopped."

"Wait a second. What else can we figure out?"

"How about: If the entire floor is wet, then it was just

mopped *and* we know the janitor was just here."

Double check!

The rest of the hunt went quickly. When they finished, the boys plopped down at a table at the back of the math classroom. The final prompt was to write some "If, Then" statements of their own.

Gabriel started scribbling away.

Thomas paused for a moment and then realized something. Logic wasn't just for wet floors and water fountains; he could use it in his search to prove God's existence!

Thomas slipped out his detective notebook to write a few notes.

Why It Is Logical That There Is a God:

Answer to the first clue: **If** everything was somehow first moved by someone else, **then** at some point there had to be an Original Mover (God).

Answer to the second clue: **If** everything was made by someone/something else, **then** at some point there had to be a First Cause.

"YES!" Thomas exclaimed so loudly it made Gabriel jump.

Thomas re-entered the classroom with an enthusiastic "Wow, thanks Mr. Baker!"

Mr. Baker looked surprised but pleased. "You're welcome, Thomas. From now on, I'll bet you use logic every day of your life."

Thomas smiled. He was starting to make some real progress with his mystery.

He counted down the minutes until the end of class so he could get to the next clue.

Chapter 8
Death and Other Mysteries

Standing at his locker at the end of the day, Thomas opened the box again. The object inside this time made him jump in alarm.

"Fish food! Oh man, I forgot to feed my fish!"

"How long's it been?" asked Gabriel, grabbing his backpack from a locker nearby.

"Too long," groaned Thomas, guiltily staring at the

small container of fish food.

Thomas wasn't sure what this had to do with proving God's existence, but he knew he had to feed Roley, right away. It had been at least two days since he had fed his pet.

"Catch you later, Gabe. I'm hoping I get home in time to save Roley!" Thomas called over his shoulder as he pushed open the school's big double doors to head home.

Despite his hopes, Thomas was worried. He couldn't think about anything else for the whole car ride home.

"Tom, let's play basketball when we get home," Charlie suggested. "Whoever wins doesn't have to help with dinner dishes!"

"Sure, but I have to feed Roley first." Thomas was feeling more and more concerned.

"And Thomas," his mom jumped in, "you were also going to do some gardening with Dad when he gets home."

"Yes, I will, after I feed my fish," Thomas assured her.

The car rolled to a stop, and Thomas jumped right out. He flew straight to the fishbowl in the living room and opened the container of fish food.

Then he stopped and looked. Roley was acting funny. Instead of swimming, he was floating on his side, not moving.

Dead. His pet fish was dead. And it was his fault.

Thomas sank down onto the couch. He was responsible for Roley's food, and he hadn't fed him for days.

How could he forget something so important? Thomas hated that he got so distracted all the time! He wiped a couple of tears off his face.

After a few minutes, Mom walked into the room. She looked at the fish tank. She looked at Thomas. Then she sat beside him without saying a word.

"Mom," Thomas said, "I can't believe Roley is dead!

I wish I could tell him how sorry I am that I forgot to feed him."

His mom gave him a quick hug and looked him in the eye. "I'm sorry you lost your pet, Thomas. It is a hard lesson to learn. Every living creature and plant depends on something else to live. The plants need sunlight and water (that's why it's Anna's job to water our plants). Your fish needed food. But we all mess up sometimes! You're becoming a big kid, and with that, it means you are learning about responsibility."

Thomas sniffed back a tear or two. "Do you forgive me, Mom? Do you think one day we can get another pet? I promise I will take better care of him or her."

His mom smiled. "Of course I forgive you! Mistakes are a part of being human. I can see that you have learned something very important today."

"Oh yes!" Thomas said. "I understand now that pets need us to be able to survive, and that if I'm going to have an animal depend on me, I'd better pay more attention.

Maybe I should set an extra alarm or something if I ever get another animal. A pet-feeding alarm!"

His mom gave him another hug. "I'm proud of you, Thomas. It's OK to be sad, and it's not an easy thing to experience. Life is so precious."

This was a tough lesson to swallow. After his mom left the room, Thomas kept thinking about his fish's death. Even though he was sad, he realized that everything is temporary.

Sitting there on the couch, Thomas suddenly decided to pray, quietly, from his heart.

"Lord, I want to know You. I want to know You exist. But to be honest, it's been a tough day. My friends don't understand me, and I let my pet die. Can You please help a guy out? Help me see what I'm supposed to learn from all of this!"

He sat quietly for a few minutes, then realized he hadn't even read the next clue. He'd been so distracted by the fish food that he forgot! He pulled the box out of his backpack and retrieved the clue. It read:

Thomas,

I'm sorry for the loss of your fish. Its existence depended on being fed. While this is a personally difficult proof for you, I challenge you to see what you can learn about God from Roley's passing.

Here's a new term for you: Roley was a **contingent being.** That means his existence depended on someone else. Actually, everything you've ever seen (including you!) is a contingent being. Think about it!

However, there must be something or Someone who brings things into existence, but whose existence doesn't rely on anything else. In Philosophy, we call that a **Necessary Being.**

Keep up your observations and see if you can discover why God is the Necessary Being.

T. A.

Reality Detective Lab

1. How do you think the fish will lead Thomas to God?

2. Can you think of an example of another **contingent being**?

3. Is a flower a contingent being?

4. Can you think of something that is not a **contingent being**?

Chapter 9
No Beginning and No End

O h boy, Thomas thought, re-reading the note. *This one doesn't seem as simple to figure out.* But he was determined to give it a go.

He looked around the room for "contingent beings" — things that depended on something else to exist.

Once he started looking, it was surprisingly easy to discover contingent beings, from his sister's artwork to

the flowers on the windowsill. He pulled his notebook
out of his backpack and began to write.

OBSERVATIONS

A list of contingent beings:

Fish: are born and die and need to be fed to keep existing (true for every living creature!)

Flowers: grow from seeds and then die, need sun and water to exist

Toys: are made by people and eventually break or wear out

Artwork: created by people and must be protected so it doesn't fall apart

I think I get the idea here, he thought. *Everything needs something else, not just to exist, but to continue existing.*

But Thomas was sort of stumped. He got that everything needed something else to keep existing, but so what? What did that have to do with God?

"Thomas?" His mother poked her head around the corner. "I think it's time to get a start on homework."

Thomas sighed. He really did like school, but when he was working on a mystery, it was hard for him to focus on anything else.

Grabbing his backpack and his detective notebook, he went into the kitchen, where Charlie was already working. Though Charlie's idea of working was sitting at the table with his math worksheets ... and three granola bars, a pile of pepperoni, and a bag of Skittles he had nicked from the pantry.

"Nice haul," Thomas said, eying Charlie's stash.

"There *might* be some more granola bars left," Charlie offered, not very helpfully. "Maybe."

Thomas rolled his eyes and grabbed himself his favorite snack — an apple, a jar of peanut butter, and a knife for spreading.

He sat down at the kitchen table and opened his backpack to grab the current book study, *Johnny Tremain*. He put his detective notebook on the table to look at later, but then had an idea. Learning about those "IF" and "THEN" statements might come in handy for solving this new clue.

Casting poor *Johnny Tremain* to an abandoned corner of the table, Thomas got a pencil and opened his class notebook to the section from today's class.

He tried out a few "IF" and "THEN" statements about contingent beings to see if anything clicked.

IF Anna draws on paper, THEN her artwork exists.

Well, that's obvious, thought Thomas. He tried the opposite:

IF Anna doesn't draw on the paper, THEN the artwork doesn't exist.

He looked around the kitchen and living room at all the furniture, toys, and plants. If no one had made these things, none of them would exist!

But what about a time before all that furniture was made, or before plants were created, or even — he looked outside — before the sun and world itself existed?

Was there a time when nothing at all existed? *Nothing*?

Thomas felt a bit dizzy.

Determined, he set pencil to paper again.

IF there was a time when nothing existed, THEN ...

Then what? All Thomas could come up with was a question:

> IF nothing existed, THEN how could contingent beings ever come into existence?
>
> Nothing comes from nothing.
>
> So something must have always existed.

Thomas had to admit that this one was a little above his head. But he knew that God is the only being he could think of who didn't need anything or anyone else to support His existence.

OK, one more time ...

> IF God always existed, THEN everything could be created by Him and depend on Him for its existence.

This clue made his brain hurt, but he thought he was finally getting somewhere.

A drawing Charlie had made at Vacation Bible School, hanging on the fridge, caught his eye. It was a painting of Moses and the burning bush. Typical Charlie — the fiery bush was massive and impressive!

Thomas had learned about the burning bush many times, but never gave it any serious thought. God appeared to Moses in the burning bush, and Moses said, "Who are you?" God replied, "I AM WHO I AM." This name means that God is existence. He is the root of everything, the reason we all exist.

Thinking of God as the only Being that is not dependent on anyone else for existence helped Thomas know God a bit better. And now, he knew the answer to this third clue.

He brought out a scrap of paper and wrote:

Proof 3: God is not dependent on anyone for His existence. But everything in the world that comes into existence ultimately depends on Him.

He closed the box, and the fish food and the piece of paper disappeared.

Chapter 10
"Anything You Can Do,
I Can Do Better"

"Hey!" Charlie interrupted Thomas's thoughts. "Let's play basketball, and if I win (which I obviously will), I don't have to help with dishes tonight. And you have to show me what's in that strange little box you're staring at."

Never able to turn down a competition, Thomas

sprang up from his chair, and they headed to the driveway.

"Are you tired yet? I could play basketball for hours," taunted Charlie.

"No way! I'm not tired at all. And I'm so much faster than you are," Thomas retorted.

"Yeah, well, I have a better shot." Charlie sank the ball in the basket to prove his point.

Thomas puffed out his chest. "I'm taller."

"I'm better."

"GOOOO, Charlie," yelled Mom in a make-believe cheerleader voice. Then, in a slightly different tone, like she was pretending to be someone else: "Thomas, Thomas, he's our man, if he can't do it, no one can."

She finished her cheers with a fake wave of fake pom-poms and — believe it or not — a real cartwheel.

"MOMMM!!" both boys groaned together.

"You can't cheer for both of us," said Thomas.

"Yeah," Charlie chimed in. "You have to cheer for

86

me, because I'm better at basketball."

"Boys, you know you don't always have to compare. You could just play for fun!"

"OK, Mom," they chorused as she turned to head inside.

Charlie waited a moment and then whispered loudly to Thomas, "I really am the better basketball player."

Before Thomas could respond, Charlie tossed the ball into the basket to prove his point. "SCORE!" Charlie yelled. "Time to take a look at that secret box of yours."

Resigned, Thomas headed inside and grabbed the box, and the two boys went upstairs and flopped on Thomas's bed.

Charlie snatched the box and opened the note inside. Quickly scanning it, he exclaimed, "What's with the poem?"

Thomas took the note and read aloud:

Dear Thomas,

Nice, nicer, nicest —
Tell me who is the best?
Smart, smarter, smartest —
Talent put to the test.
When you compare,
Do you consider (or care)
Who is really the best out there?

T. A.

P.S. When we compare people, places, and things,
we describe them by different levels of qualities like
"good, better, and best." My question for you is: Is there
Someone out there who has every good quality perfectly?

Reality Detective Lab

1. Think of the nicest person you know. Can you imagine a person even nicer?

2. What are some other qualities we find in the world to different degrees?

3. Can you think of a perfect example of one of these qualities? If so, can you imagine the possibility of a more perfect example?

4. Things and people can always be more perfect. They could always have *more* of some quality. How will this reality help Thomas understand how we can know God exists?

"OK, what is going on here? Are you working on some sort of mystery again?" Charlie asked.

"Yeah, and this time, it's about the biggest question of them all!" Thomas gave Charlie a quick rundown of all that had happened since Mateo challenged him at the baseball game.

For once, Charlie didn't have a joking response. A little stunned, he finally asked, "What now?"

Thomas got down to business. He wrote in his notebook:

OBSERVATION

People will always be better at certain things than others.

Charlie looked over his shoulder. "Like I'll always be better at basketball!"

"I'm going to ignore that comment, Charlie. Here's the thing, it's not just basketball that has different levels of qualities, it's everything."

Charlie made a silly smooching face. "Like prettiness. We all know you think Beth in your class isn't just pretty, she's the prettiest girl in the whole world."

"So what? She *is* really pretty." Thomas blushed.

"But is she the prettiest girl in the whole entire world?"

Thomas hesitated. Could he really say she was the absolute prettiest? He didn't like to admit it, but there probably was a girl somewhere, sometime, who was even more beautiful.

"I don't know that I could ever say someone is the prettiest ever, the smartest ever, or the nicest ever," Thomas concluded. "It seems like there could always be someone out there who was even prettier, smarter, or nicer."

Looking out his bedroom window, Thomas spotted

his dad getting ready to garden. Quick to escape when it came to chores, Charlie scooted out of the room, while Thomas made his way to the garage to find his gardening gloves and prepare to pick weeds. Fun. Fun. Fun.

On the upside, he had some time to pick his dad's brain about his newest clue.

"Dad," Thomas began as he pulled on his gloves, "who would you say is the smartest person on earth?

"Well ..." his dad started, "I would say the smartest guy on earth is ... me!"

Thomas groaned.

"OK, just kidding. I think the people who invent technological devices like iPhones are smart."

"Are they the smartest people ever?" Thomas persisted. "What about Einstein?"

"He was also brilliant," Dad agreed. He paused for a moment. "Why are you asking, Thomas?"

Thomas focused on pulling out a particularly stubborn weed. It came out with a huge yank. "What

I'm wondering is ... I know we can say people or things are better or worse than others, but is anything *perfect*?"

Dad chuckled. "What are they teaching you in school? Those are some big thoughts. Let me ask you this. What is perfection, then, if it's something nobody has?"

Thomas thought of Beth's prettiness, the intelligence of people like Aristotle, and his brother's basketball skills (groan!), and realized they all had something in common.

"God," he said aloud.

His dad looked up from his gardening, a little bit surprised.

Thomas continued, "God made us. He gave us all our gifts. If He can give them to us, He must have them perfectly Himself. God is perfect!"

"Wow, Thomas, are they teaching you logic at school? That's incredible reasoning."

"Something like that," said Thomas sheepishly.

"Look at these flowers. God's perfect beauty is reflected in them. In fact, all of creation has some level of perfection and points us to Him."

Thomas was satisfied. Together, he and his dad finished the weeding, giving those beautiful flowers more room to grow.

Pausing to gulp down some water, Thomas returned to the gold box. He took out a piece of paper and wrote:

Proof 4: All good qualities are levels that reach for a standard of perfection. Therefore, perfection must exist. That perfection is God.

He closed the box and headed for the kitchen, whistling as he went.

Chapter 11
The Great Design

Thomas walked into the kitchen; all this sleuthing was giving him an appetite! It was getting close to dinner time, but he spotted some freshly baked peanut butter cookies and helped himself to one.

Anna came into the room and immediately spied Thomas's cookie. "Hey! You could have asked before you took a cookie. They didn't just make themselves, you know!"

"Hmm, that's true, a cookie can't make itself."

Anna snatched the cookie triumphantly, added it back to the batch, and covered them all up.

"Mom and I made them! They're for after dinner."

"Fine." Thomas grinned. He could wait. After all, he only had one more clue to solve!

"Here it goes." He opened the box and found one of the cookies Anna just baked.

Thomas looked up at Anna. "Anna, did you sneak a cookie into this box for me?"

"Noooo, I already told you they're for dessert." She opened the sliding door to the backyard and headed for the swings.

As he got ready to read the note, he took a big bite of the cookie. Solving the biggest question of the universe was hard work!

Dear Thomas,

Last clue! Are you feeling more confident that you can rationally affirm God's existence yet?

Everything in existence is created for a purpose. Even that cookie!

Yet these things didn't come up with these goals by themselves or by chance. Do you think that something or Someone had to give them their purpose?

You know what to do from here!

T. A.

Thomas actually wasn't sure if he knew what to do from here. He took another bite of the cookie.

Out of ideas, he stepped outside and called, "Hey Anna, what's the purpose of a cookie?"

"Are you crazy, Tom? The purpose is to be something delicious!" Anna called down from her swing.

Thomas thought some more. "And the purpose of cookie dough?"

"To make a cookie, obviously! I mean, unless you eat it straight from the bowl."

"OK, so what you're saying is, cookie dough has a purpose. It's a purpose we gave it: to become a cookie."

"Everything has a purpose," Anna replied, a bit impatiently.

"Oh yeah? What about those seeds we're going to plant in the flower bed?"

"They'll become beautiful flowers."

"Are you telling me a seed doesn't ever become a lion?" Thomas joked.

Reality Detective Lab

1. What is the purpose of a seed? What does it become?

2. Does a flower seed know how to become a flower all by itself?

3. We know many living things work together to nourish life in the universe. Who designed them to be that way?

Anna just shook her head and kept swinging.

Thomas took out his notebook and started to write down some thoughts.

OBSERVATIONS

1. Seeds become flowers (or other plants).

2. A flower seed ALWAYS becomes a flower. It doesn't ever become something else.

Thomas put down his pencil to think. How do seeds know to become flowers? They don't even have brains!

"What else do seeds accomplish when they become flowers?"

Thomas didn't realize he had asked the question out loud until Anna replied.

"They are beautiful so we can enjoy them!"

Charlie came up behind Thomas, startling him. "Flowers provide pollen for bees, seeds for new flowers, and sometimes they even have medicinal qualities."

"Geez, Charlie, how do you know all this stuff?" Thomas asked good-naturedly.

"Flowers also provide bees with pollen and nectar to eat. Then, of course, bees create honey, which humans and bears eat," Charlie said, now sitting on the other swing and trying to reach higher in the sky than Anna.

"That's really amazing," Thomas said. "A seed has all those purposes in it from the very beginning. And the whole universe is like the bees and the flowers, working together to create one incredible world!"

"God created the whole world," Anna said, reaching the heart of the question without realizing it.

It was true. Suddenly, thinking about every leaf that grows, every web that is spun, and every baby that is born, Thomas saw a great Creator's hand.

With a flourish, Thomas took out a last scrap of paper and wrote:

Proof 5: Because even things without brains work toward goals they don't choose but pursue naturally, it is reasonable that there is a First Designer that gave them those goals. That First Designer is God.

He had devoured the cookie from the box, so Thomas walked over and got a seed from the pile waiting to be planted. He placed the seed and the note in the box, and FLASH! Not only did they disappear, but the box disappeared, too.

In its place was one final letter.

Chapter 12
At the Heart of It All

Dear Thomas,

You truly are a great detective! We were made for God and for seeking the truth. Now, you have begun that quest!

You have discovered five clues to God's existence. I wrote about these clues in my introduction to theology: the **Summa Theologiae.** (Don't let the Latin scare you — it means "Summary of Theology," and theology is the study of God.)

As you have seen, even 11-year-olds can begin to uncover why it is reasonable to assume that God exists. Here are the proofs you discovered:

Proof 1: Everything that changes or moves does so because of something else. There must be, therefore, someone who does not change but who moves everything else. This Unmoved Mover is God.

Proof 2: **IF** everything was made by someone or something else, **THEN** at some point there had to be a First Maker or Cause.

Proof 3: Everything and everyone we see in the world depends on something or someone else for their existence — they are contingent beings. But in order for them to exist, something or Someone must exist who doesn't depend on anyone else to exist. That is God.

Proof 4: All good qualities are levels (such as being smart, smarter, or the smartest) that reach for a standard of perfection. Perfection is God.

Proof 5: Because even things without brains work toward natural purposes, it is reasonable that there is a First Designer.

God is real, and we can discover that God is real with our reason!

Don't let anyone tell you that faith and reason are opposed. In fact, they work together. But these five proofs are just the beginning. Knowing that God exists is one thing; knowing Him is another.

You have been wondering who I am. My name is Thomas Aquinas, and during my life (a long time ago, in the thirteenth century), I was a theologian. I wrote and taught about who God is.

After many years of writing and teaching, I stopped. When a friend asked me why, I explained to him that all my knowledge about the Lord was nothing compared to my **experience** of Him.

So, while reason has its place and is very important, before you put down your detective notebook, I urge you to do one final thing: Go find Jesus. He is waiting for you.

Signed,

Thomas Aquinas

? ❓ ?

"Mom, I know it's near dinner time, but could you drive me up to church for a few minutes?"

Thomas's mom looked like she was going to faint from surprise. (OK, OK, so sometimes he wasn't that enthusiastic about going to church.)

"Is everything OK, Thomas?" she asked uncertainly.

"Yeah, I just ... need to figure something out.'"

Mom put down the vegetables she had been slicing for dinner and grabbed the keys.

"Honey, I'm running out quickly with Thomas.

We'll be right back," she called.

One of Thomas's favorite things about his mom was that she didn't force him to talk. She just put on a little music, and they hummed along together as they rode to the church.

Thomas Aquinas, Thomas thought. Wow. Thomas had always heard that saints cared about him, but there's nothing like seeing that intercession in action! Come to think of it, Thomas Aquinas was Thomas's patron saint. No wonder he was so interested in helping Thomas figure out his proofs for God's existence.

When they got to the familiar church, something seemed different. Thomas knew the church well from Sunday Mass, but today there was no organ playing, no cars in the parking lot, and no little kids tugging on their parents' sleeves asking them if there would be donuts afterwards. Thomas and his mom went inside. He moved to sit in a pew up front while his mom looked at the bulletin in the vestibule.

Come closer.

Thomas heard those words, not aloud, but in his heart. He was sure of it. He looked around again at the empty church, but there was no one else there.

Then his eyes were drawn to the tabernacle, and he suddenly realized the church wasn't empty. Jesus was there. In the tabernacle. Waiting for him.

His heart pounding in excitement, Thomas walked to the front of the church, genuflected, and knelt at the altar rail where some parishioners chose to receive Holy Communion on their knees.

He bowed his head to pray. "Uh, I'm here, Lord."

Silence.

"I came because the letter told me to come. Because, well, because I've been trying to find out if it's logical that You exist. And guess what? It is! Oh, I guess You already knew that. What I'm trying to say is, I'm glad I went on this journey."

Thomas knelt in silence for a few minutes.

Again, in his heart, he heard: *I am glad that you are here. I will always be here for you. I am the First Mover and the First Cause. I am also Father, Son, and Holy Spirit. I want true joy for your life, Thomas.*

Thomas sat in God's Presence.

With a sense of awe and renewed understanding, Thomas said a prayer of thanksgiving and stood up to leave the church.

As he walked back down the center aisle, he glanced up at the stained-glass windows and saw something he had never noticed before. One of the windows depicted a man writing at a desk, using a feather pen. The feather seemed to point to the label at the bottom of the frame. Thomas stepped a bit closer to read it: St. Thomas Aquinas.

He smiled from ear to ear. His new friend had been present in his home church all these years!

Chapter 13
Play Ball

The next day, after school, Thomas threw on his baseball uniform and headed out the door. It was a perfect afternoon. A couple of clouds floated in the sky, but lots of sunshine filtered through the leafy trees. A good day to play ball.

"Thanks, God," Thomas said. Thanks to Thomas Aquinas, he had a new understanding that such a beautiful day was only possible because of God's existence.

He reached the field only to find Mateo waiting with his glove and a ball to warm up.

"So? Did you figure out how we can know if God exists?" Mateo threw the ball to Thomas.

Thomas caught it and got ready to throw it back. "You know, I actually did, with a bit of help."

"You mean the clues in that box?"

"Yeah, exactly."

A bit of Mateo's joking nature crept back into the conversation. "So you're saying now you know the answer to all the big questions in the universe? What about whether Jesus exists? Or whether miracles really happen? Or, why it possibly makes sense to believe that your Communion is God?"

Thomas stopped for a moment and looked Mateo in the eye.

"I'm *not* saying I understand everything. I know

there are a lot of mysteries yet to be solved. But I also know that God is a God of faith *and* reason. I'll never know Him perfectly during my life on earth. He is God, after all! But I know I can come to know Him better."

Mateo looked a bit ashamed. "I'm sorry, Tom. I can tell this is important to you. And the truth is, I care about the answers to these questions, too."

"You do?"

"How about we make a deal? You explain to me how we can know that God exists sometime, but for now, we both just concentrate on winning this game!"

"Deal!"

Just at that moment, the umpire called out, "OK, players, let's play ball!"

With that, Thomas tipped his hat silently to his namesake St. Thomas Aquinas, picked up his mitt, and hit the field.

Discussion Questions

Reflect on these questions and talk about your answers with your parents!

* Have you ever had questions about why we believe in God and our Catholic Faith?

* Which one of the five proofs for God's existence makes the most sense to you? (There is no wrong answer!)

* Would you feel comfortable explaining that proof

to a friend? Why or why not?

* Which proof is the most difficult for you to understand? Once you've identified which one, ask your parents or even your parish priest to explain it more to you!

* As Thomas Aquinas told Thomas, it's natural to want to know more! What are some questions you have about our Catholic Faith?

* At the end of the story, Thomas spends quiet time with God in his parish church. Did you know that you can stop by your church and pray like that? Jesus is always there waiting for you in the tabernacle! Ask your parents if you can stop by one day like Thomas did.

Who was St. Thomas Aquinas?

Born: 1226

Died: 1274

Feast Day: January 28

Patron saint of all students and universities

St. Thomas Aquinas wrote a lot during his life. His *Summa Theologiae*, in which he wrote his five proofs for God's existence, is a brilliant summary of theology.

Today, he is known as a Doctor of the Church alongside other great saints such as Saint Augustine and St. Thérèse of Lisieux. But of course, once upon a time (in the thirteenth century — the 1230s, to be exact), he was a boy just like Detective Thomas.

Thomas Aquinas was the youngest of nine siblings. His father was the Count of Aquino in Italy. When Thomas was only five years old, he was sent to study with the monks at Monte Cassino. He was known to be a smart kid and was reported to continually ask grownups, "What is God?"

Thomas Aquinas went on to study at university. He became a Dominican friar when he was not yet twenty years old. Dominican friars were very poor. His family was not happy about this, so they kidnapped him and kept him trapped in a fortress for an entire year!

Still, Aquinas stayed faithful to his calling, and his family eventually gave up and let him go.

Aquinas went on to study under another incredible

St. Thomas Aquinas

thinker, St. Albert the Great. We know now that Aquinas was brilliant, but because he was very quiet in class and didn't brag about being smart, some other students thought he wasn't. They even gave him a mean nickname: "The Dumb Ox."

Aquinas didn't let what other people thought bother him. He spent his adult life traveling, studying, writing, and teaching people about God. Eventually, everyone realized he was anything but dumb. An important part of his life's work was to show people that natural knowledge and reasoning are perfectly compatible with the things God has revealed to us.

In other words, faith and reason go together. As Detective Thomas found out, we can know that God exists just by using our reason!

When he was forty-nine years old, Aquinas fell ill and died. His legacy, however, is still serving the Church and the world more than 700 years later.

St. Thomas Aquinas, pray for us!

About the Author

Caitlin Bootsma started believing in the transformative power of stories when her dad first read her *The Chronicles of Narnia* at age four. Caitlin's own story includes degrees in theology and communication, including a graduate degree earned in Rome, and over fifteen years of experience in Catholic communications. Today, Caitlin serves as her parish's librarian and is the wife to a church architect and the mom to five inquisitive kids, who provide a lot of inspiration for her writings! You can follow Caitlin at www.instagram.com/theinkyswan.

About the Illustrator

Evie Faith Schwartzbauer is a Minneapolis-based artist who creates illustrations and logo designs and does face painting. A convert to the Catholic Faith, Evie is a passionate advocate for authentic Catholicism and the pro-life cause. You can find Evie and her work online at behance.net /evieRombalArt, and on Instagram @evierombal.